ABOUT CECELIA

Before embarking on her writing career, Cecelia Ahern completed a degree in Journalism and Media Communications. At twenty-one years old, she wrote her first novel, *PS I Love You* which instantly became an international bestseller and was adapted into a major motion picture starring Hilary Swank. Her successive novels, *Where Rainbows End, If You Could See Me Now, A Place Called Here, Thanks for the Memories, The Gift* and *The Book of Tomorrow* were all number one bestsellers. Her books are published in forty-six countries and have collectively sold over ten million copies. Cecelia has also co-created the hit ABC Network comedy series *Samantha Who?* which stars Christina Applegate. In 2008 Cecelia won the award for the Best New Writer at the Glamour Women of the Year Awards. Cecelia lives in Dublin, Ireland.

To sign up for the exclusive Cecelia Ahern HarperCollins newsletter and discover all about Cecelia's books, as well as interviews, photographs and much more, log onto **www.cecelia-ahern.com**

PS – don't forget to read Cecelia's other novels:

P.S. I Love You
Where Rainbows End
If You Could See Me Now
A Place Called Here
Thanks for the Memories
The Gift
The Book of Tomorrow

CECELIA AHERN

Girl in the Mirror

HarperCollins*Publishers*

HarperCollinsPublishers
77–85 Fulham Palace Road,
Hammersmith, London W6 8JB

www.harpercollins.co.uk

Published by HarperCollinsPublishers 2011

1

A catalogue record for this book
is available from the British Library

ISBN: 978 0 00 742503 7

Typeset in by Palimpsest Book Production Limited, Grangemouth,
Stirlingshire

Printed and bound in Great Britain by Clays Ltd, St Ives plc

For my Fairy Godmother, Sarah Kelly

'There's no use trying,' she said. 'One can't believe impossible things.' (Alice)

'I daresay you haven't had much practice,' said the Queen. 'When I was younger, I always did it for half an hour a day. Why, sometimes I believed as many as six impossible things before breakfast."

Alice's Adventures in Wonderland

Girl in the Mirror

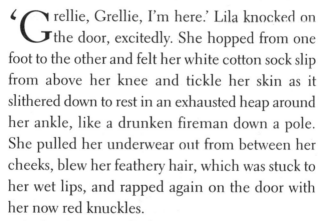

'Grellie, Grellie, I'm here.' Lila knocked on the door, excitedly. She hopped from one foot to the other and felt her white cotton sock slip from above her knee and tickle her skin as it slithered down to rest in an exhausted heap around her ankle, like a drunken fireman down a pole. She pulled her underwear out from between her cheeks, blew her feathery hair, which was stuck to her wet lips, and rapped again on the door with her now red knuckles.

'Why do you call her Grellie?' the little girl beside her finally spoke up. Her voice was tiny beside the gigantic front door. She noticed that and moved closer to Lila for safety. Protection against what she wasn't sure.

The front garden they had walked through was

a jungle; untamed and unkempt, not like Sarah's garden at all, where their gardener came every two weeks to make sure everything was symmetrical and perfect, and winked at her whenever he saw her at the window. She would marry him if she was old enough. But this garden was different. She felt she'd have gotten lost for ever if she'd stepped off the randomly placed flagstones that led to the front door. The deep-scented wild flowers stretched above her, all nosy to see inside the house as though they were fighting for space. The trees' branches arched out and contorted in such disturbing angles they made Sarah shudder.

'Grellie,' Lila rapped again, impatiently.

'Stop calling her that,' Sarah said, nervously then. 'Why do you keep calling her that?'

Lila finally picked up on her nerves and stopped jittering to look at her curiously. She became defensive, her eyes narrowed. 'She's my grandma Ellie. I call her Grellie.'

'Oh. Well maybe she's not here. Maybe we should just go.'

Sensing an opportunity to leave, Sarah quickly spun around and prepared to step onto the first mouldy flagstone, but her pulse quickened again when she heard the bolt of the giant door slide back and creak so loud it was as though they'd awakened a sleeping giant from a hundred-year slumber.

'Grellie!' Lila yelped excitedly, and Sarah said a silent goodbye to the front gate for now.

Lila was embraced warmly by a grey-haired woman. The front of her hair was pure white and it was pinned back in a bun. She had a cane in her hand, which was behind Lila's back as she squeezed her. The hug looked warm. Inviting. Sarah's nerves dissolved a little.

'Well aren't you an impatient little thing today?' Ellie laughed and peeled herself away from her granddaughter. 'I was down the back of the garden, weeding, I could hear you all the way.'

'I thought you weren't here, I thought you'd forgotten,' Lila said breathlessly.

'Of course I hadn't forgotten. How could I forget I'd be meeting your very special friend today. I've been excited to meet her all day.'

Sarah smiled, her cheeks pinked.

Ellie's voice was hard, and she spoke as if something was catching in her throat, something trapped in there.

Sarah couldn't help herself listening to that trapped something. She cleared her throat.

Ellie looked directly at her. Sarah smiled.

'This is Sarah,' Lila said proudly. 'Sarah, this is Grellie.'

Sarah didn't know whether to smile or not. She did.

'Hi.' Her voice was tiny again.

'Well hello, Sarah, you're very welcome. Why don't you both come in out of the chill and see what I've prepared for you.' She turned and went into the house. Lila disappeared after her, hopping up and down with excitement.

'Did you make your fairy cakes? With the pink icing? Did you put the marshmallow on the cake? Did you make the cake? Did you make your strawberry jam? I told Sarah you make your own and she didn't believe me. Did you make some for the scones? Do the scones have fruit? I'd love clotted cream with them if you did.'

Lila gabbered on and on in a giddy hysteria while Sarah stood outside the front door listening to the crash of the waves against the steep cliffs below. It was a beautiful sunny day. It was July and school had just finished for the summer and everyone had been excited. Class had been taken outside and all they'd done was read a story and then had a party on the grass. On the journey to Ellie's house everybody's car windows had been open and Sarah had listened to the mix of music and chat drift out the windows and fuse in the sky to confuse the passing birds.

But here was different. Here it felt cold.

Sarah looked at the gate again; she'd left it slightly open. A gap large enough for a ginger cat to creep in. As though sensing her gaze, it stopped, arched its back and looked at her. They both stayed like that for a while.

'Sarah, where are you?'

Sarah snapped to attention.

'There you are.' Lila appeared at the front door. 'What are you doing?'

'I was just …' Tell her, tell her you want to leave.

'Oh that's Gingersnap. Grellie!' Lila shouted at the top of her lungs.

'I'm not deaf, my dear!' Ellie called back.

'Gingersnap is back!'

She heard Grellie call something back but didn't know what she said but heard the something in her throat.

Sarah cleared hers again.

'Come on, wait till you see,' Lila said, eyes bright.

She grabbed Sarah's hand and pulled her inside

and they both laughed as Sarah allowed herself to be tugged. The entrance hall was large. Its vastness severed Sarah's laughter and made her stop suddenly in her tracks and, in turn, stopped Lila. Sarah looked around. There was a fireplace in the hallway. A chandelier. Dusty, a web or two draped

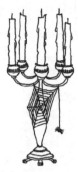

from one candelabra to another, which occasionally shimmered when the sunlight hit it. The floorboards were worn, chipped and uneven, and creaked beneath even the lightest tiptoe. It was clear to see what they once looked like from the edges of the room. A polished border. Above the dark wooden fireplace stood two lonely candlesticks devoid of candles. And above them a black sheet was draped over something to reveal only its brass frame.

'What's the picture of?' Sarah asked, uncertainty returning to her.

'What picture?' Lila asked confused.

'The one above the fireplace.'

'That's not a picture, it's a black sheet,' Lila said, as though Sarah were mad.

'What's beneath the sheet?'

Lila grabbed her hand and pulled her again.

'A mirror. Grellie doesn't like mirrors. Come on, let me show you around. We can have loads of adventures.'

Lila showed Sarah around the house with excitement, opening doors and announcing the room's purpose and function and possible adventure before swiftly closing them again and running off with Sarah in tow.

The house was certainly grand, as Lila had promised, the ceilings high, the windows covering floor to ceiling, lots of knick-knacks, lots of hiding places. Lots of dark places. Lila didn't seem to notice. To her the house was filled with colour, delight, mystery and her memories. But where Lila saw light, Sarah saw the shadows, where Lila felt warmth, Sarah felt the chill. Each new room Sarah saw was colder than the previous. Each room had full walls, or sections of the wall, covered in black sheets. They leered at Sarah like the Grim Reaper.

They ran past a door and, unusually, Lila didn't fling it open.

'What's in there?' Sarah asked.

Lila stopped running. 'Oh.' She leaned over the banister and looked downstairs to see if Grellie was near. They could hear her clattering plates in the kitchen. 'I'm not allowed in there but I'll show you.'

'No, it's okay. I don't want to go in if you're not allowed,' Sarah said, backing away.

'I'll show you.' Lila smiled. 'It's no big deal. It's just a spare room.'

'Then why aren't you allowed in?'

Lila just shrugged. 'I've never asked why but I've been in here loads of times.'

She reached up and lifted the key off the top of the doorframe where it was hidden, put it in the keyhole and turned. All the time, Sarah's heart raced and she looked around expecting Ellie to appear beside them at any moment, even though they could hear her downstairs.

'No, Lila, don't. I don't want to get into trouble.'

'We won't,' Lila whispered.

She pushed the door open and Sarah waited for something to jump out at her but it didn't. Nothing happened. It was a boring room. A double bed, off-white bedding, two bed-side lockers, a fireplace. But what dominated the room was a full-length, free-standing mirror, which was draped completely in black.

Sarah swallowed. It wasn't the biggest piece in the room but it was imposing, it seemed to take over the room.

'Let's go in,' Lila whispered.

'No.' Sarah pulled her back. She tried to hide the terror from her voice and attempted a smile but felt her lips tremble. 'I want to see all the lovely cakes you were telling me about.'

Lila lit up as though she'd forgotten. She locked the door and they ran downstairs, through what felt like dozens of rooms and ended up in the conservatory. Lila displayed the spread proudly. She hadn't lied. The table was filled with cakes, biscuits, scones and pies and all homemade if the pots and pans in the sink were anything to go by. Fruits spilled out of bowls and blobs of cream lazily sprawled themselves in containers dotted around the table. Jugs of juices, lemonades, no doubt homemade too.

But around this beautiful vision the garden was fighting to get inside. Trees reached out their branches like arms, twigs like claws, clinging to the side of the glass. The flowers and their pretty, colourful faces looked ghostly, evil almost as they glared in at the food, at Sarah, at all of them, watching, waiting for something to happen. What weeding Ellie had claimed to be doing was beyond Sarah. She couldn't see how she could step outside of the house without being lost for ever.

'Well? What do you think?' Lila asked.

Ellie was standing beside the table, cane in hand, the tip lodged between the crack in the terracotta tiles.

Sarah's voice was even smaller in this room as she said, 'I'd like to go home now.'

'What?' Lila asked in shock. 'Why?'

Sarah ignored Lila and looked at Ellie. 'I'd like to go home now please,' she said again politely.

'I'll call your mother,' Ellie said calmly, as if expecting this to happen.

'But why?' Lila looked from Grellie to Sarah as though there was something they both knew but weren't sharing with her. 'Are you sick? Do you not like fairy cakes. You don't have to eat them.'

'Come Lila,' Ellie said gently. 'Give Sarah some

space now. I'd expect you'd like to wait for your mother at the gate?'

The gate. Still open a fraction. She couldn't wait to get out of there.

She nodded, then remembered her manners. 'Yes please.'

Lila and Sarah sat beside one another on the wall, kicking their legs, allowing their heels to bang back against the crumbling brickwork. They never spoke. Not until Sarah's mother's car was in sight.

'Thank you for inviting me,' Sarah said politely, feeling relieved.

'You didn't have fun. You were hardly here for very long. I didn't even get to show you my hiding place in the back garden.'

Sarah shuddered. She hopped off the wall as the car slowed to a stop beside them and she offered Lila a warm hug.

'See you over the summer?' Lila asked.

Sarah nodded.

But they didn't.

Sarah waved at her friend from the passenger seat, careful not to look at the house. It was bad luck, she remembered.

'What happened, sweetheart, did you have a fight?' her mother asked.

Sarah shook her head.

'Do you feel ill?'

She shook her head again.

Her mother reached out and felt her forehead, 'You don't feel hot.'

'I'm not.'

'Did something happen?' she asked with more urgency now and Sarah knew she'd have to explain or she'd never stop asking her. She'd even send her father to her room when he got home from work, to ask questions in a roundabout back to front way that was always so obvious to Sarah even though they thought she didn't know their true intentions.

So she spoke.

'All the mirrors were covered up with black sheets. Every mirror in every single room. All with black sheets.'

Her mother was silent. Thoughtful.

'Were they decorating?'

She shook her head. 'Lila said her grandmother doesn't like mirrors.'

Her mother was quiet, then full of false perkiness,

'Well there you go, her grandmother just doesn't like mirrors. People like different things, Sarah, you'll learn that as you go through life, it won't always make sense but that's the way it is.'

'Why wouldn't she like them?'

'Maybe she just doesn't like seeing herself, sweetheart. Some people are just like that.'

'But, Mum, it can't be the reason.'

'Why not?'

'Because her grandmother is blind.' And she lowered her voice to a whisper even though they were far from the house. 'She doesn't have any eyes.'

Lila didn't know why her Grellie didn't like mirrors, she just grew up knowing that she didn't, just like she knew not to put sugar in her father's tea and like she knew never to make her mother sit in the middle of a row at the cinema or restaurant. She didn't know why her father didn't like sweet tea or why her mother suffered a minor form of claustrophobia, she just knew that they did and that was enough information for her.

All Grellie ever said was, 'It was the price of freedom,' not that it made any sense to anybody or explained the mystery for anybody. Not only did Lila not know why but she didn't think it was odd. So the mirrors were covered with black sheeting, so the rooms were darker than most peoples' rooms. She didn't mind not knowing why her fatherdidn't take sugar in his tea or why her mother felt that the walls were closing in around her everytime she sat in the middle of a row. Even though Sarah had left the house in a rush and she subsequently heard rumours at school about her weird blind grandmother who was afraid of mirrors who lived alone in a house on a cliff, she could go the rest of her life not knowing and not caring.

But.

She should have asked.

JULY 2010

'Stop calling me.' Lila laughed down her mobile phone. 'It's bad luck or something to talk to each other.'

'It's bad luck to see each other and that's a load of crap too,' Jeremy replied. 'I just got worried you weren't going to show up. You weren't answering your phone.'

'I wasn't answering the phone because I knew it was you and it's bad luck. And of course I'm going to show up, would you stop worrying?'

'It's not bad luck and I wasn't worrying till you didn't answer the phone.'

They both laughed.

'Hold on, I'm on the road to Grellie's, I need to concentrate, I'm putting you on speakerphone.'

'Anyone in the car with you?'

'Just me and the dress.'

'Hello, dress, can't wait for you to be on the hotel bedroom floor tonight.'

Lila laughed. 'For the amount it cost me I'm never taking it off. I better go, I'm down the Bishop's Gap.'

'That's your business,' Jeremy joked as everybody always did about the steep terrain en route to Ellie's property. 'But one more thing before you go. Take a deep breath first.'

Lila groaned in advance.

'The hotel manager called. He thinks the ballroom would look more exquisite – his word not mine – if the mirrors were left as they are.'

'No. I didn't spend all that money on black fabric to not cover them up. And Grellie's bedroom – is he planning on uncovering the mirrors in there, too?'

'No, he's okay with the bedroom, it's just the ballroom. He'd like the guests to see the room properly.'

'It's my bloody wedding not his.'

Silence. Then.

'Honey … she won't even know.'

'Jeremy.'

'Sorry.'

'I can't believe you even said that.'

'I know, I take it back. I'm sorry.'

'Well in that case I'm putting goat's cheese back on the menu so your mother can be cured of her imaginary allergy to it,' Lila fumed.

'Lila. Calm down. I said I'm sorry. I know. I completely understand. I adore Ellie as much as you do. I was just trying to look at a bad situation positively.'

'There is no bad situation. Call him back and tell him he's to put the curtains back up or I'm doing it myself.'

'Okay, I'll do it. Now calm down and concentrate on that road.'

Lila calmed herself, waited for her blood to stop boiling.

'Well, two hours from now, you'll be my wife,' he said, and she could hear the smile in his voice.

'Then I can reveal my true colours and stop acting like this perfect saint now that I've snared my man,' she said, then laughed evilly.

He laughed. 'This is you as a saint?'

She smiled. Looked at herself in her mirror. She looked happy. She was happy. Had never been so happy.

'I love you, monkey,' he said.

'I love you, hippo,' she said, smiling at herself in the mirror.

She hung up just as Grellie's house came into view and the excitement rushed through her. She couldn't think of anybody more appropriate to spend the special morning with and also to accompany her up the aisle.

The front door was open before the engine had stopped and though she couldn't yet see Grellie through the wild garden, she could sense her excitement too. It drifted out from the black-and-white weather-beaten arch above the door, through the bluebells and nettles, hydrangea and dandelions. It skipped over the cracked, randomly dotted flagstones in the grass and greeted her at the creaking gate, which hung from one hinge.

She carried the dress over her arms as though carrying an exhausted sleeping child home. As soon as she neared Grellie she held the dress out.

Grellie's hands automatically reached out and felt for the fabric. Her old fingers moved gracefully like a ballet dancer on point, over the silk.

'It's ivory,' Lila whispered, not wanting sound to take away from Grellie's senses.

Grellie was quiet as her fingers inspected the dress. Lila closed her eyes, listened to the waves crashing below, and the wind's effect on the overgrowth and if she wasn't about to marry the man she loved, she almost would have wished for that moment to be frozen in time.

Grellie's fingers moved across the fabric like a concert pianist and as soon as she had finished her piece her fingers stopped moving, she clasped them together and held them to her smiling face.

'It's beautiful,' she said.

Lila hung the dress up in Grellie's bedroom and returned downstairs to the kitchen to join her. True to form, Grellie had filled the conservatory with home-baked goods.

'Grellie.' Lila laughed. 'I told you not to, I won't be able to eat this, I won't fit into my dress.'

'Oh I know,' Ellie apologised, 'I just didn't know what to do with myself so I got up at three and started baking.'

'*Three?*'

'I couldn't sleep.' She laughed. 'I'm so excited. Oh, Lila.' She grabbed her hand and held it in both of hers. They were warm from their baking duties. 'Your mum and dad would be so proud.'

'Oh don't,' Lila said, taking her hand back and wiping the corner of her eye. 'You'll ruin my make-up.'

'You have it on already?'

'Louise did my hair and make-up this morning. My hands were shaking so much I didn't trust myself,' Lila lied.

Ellie was quiet for a moment as she realised why. Of course. She would need to see her reflection to do her hair and make up.

'How do you feel about going out today?'

Ellie hadn't gone beyond the boundaries of the house's grounds for over fifity years. Since the incident.

'You know what? I feel excited.' Ellie grinned.

'I wish mum and dad could be here.'

'They will be. They'll be front row, I'm sure. Your dad was never one to miss out on a party. Front row of every feis and recital to see his girl.'

'Third best in Europe,' Lila said, and they laughed.

She was referring to the time Lila had come third in her Irish-dancing competition and her father had raved to everybody how his girl was third best in Europe. The fact of the matter was that Lila was last. Only three girls had entered the competition.

'Oh what will he be saying about me today?' Lila half laughed, half cried.

'Best bride in the church,' Ellie deepened her voice and imitated him. 'Definitely, definitely the best bride in the church.'

They both laughed.

'Oh, Grellie, what would I do without you? You're my saviour.'

'Oh and I without you my love.'

They embraced.

'Now, enough of this nonsense,' Ellie said pulling herself together. 'Let's get you into this dress before Jeremy thinks you've changed your mind.'

'Ooh,' Lila squealed with excitement, 'I'll be back in a minute.'

She ran up the dark wooden stairs breathless with excitement as she had so many years as a child, her feet landing on the worn patches in exactly the right places. She entered Grellie's bedroom and smiled at the sight of her dress hanging on the door of the wardrobe. Despite the open curtains, the room was dark. The mirror over the dresser had a black sheet over it, the full-length mirror on the wall was covered with plywood. Lila had a pang of regret that she couldn't see herself fully dressed with her hair and make-up. The first people to see her would be those in the church, she realised. She could have lipstick on her teeth for all she knew.

Well she couldn't have that. Not on her wedding day.

She went next door to the room Grellie never allowed her into; it had the best mirror in the house. A free-standing, full-length mirror. Lila had been in plenty of times but never looked in the mirror. She respected Grellie's wishes. But today was her wedding day and for the first time in twenty-eight years she was going to disobey her. If Grellie ever found out, though there was no reason why she would, then she would just explain. The most important day of her life to date. Grellie would understand. And if she didn't understand, she would forgive.

The spare bedroom had the damp smell of a room never aired, the mustiness of a room never cleaned and the iciness of a room not heated in over thirty years.

Lila felt like a naughty school girl as she pulled back the black sheet, half expecting a monster to jump out. Her heart was in her mouth. But as the fabric fell away, she was taken aback by the sight. Her. Just her. A pretty her. A beautiful her. Looking so grown up in the dress. Her eyes teared up and she felt ridiculous over such vanity. She took a step backward to get the full view. It was perfect. She felt perfect. She thought of her childhood, well and truly over now, her parents, the loss of so many things but the joy of what was to come. Silly. All over a dress.

She welled up again, laughed at herself and tried to waft air at her eyes so that the tears wouldn't fall and ruin her make-up. But it was too late. A tear ran down her cheek.

'Damn it.' She moved closer to the mirror to inspect the damage done to her eye make-up.

Smudged a little.

She did her best with her fingertips to smooth it out again. This would be her only opportunity, no more mirrors until after the church and then it would be too late.

Close up, she saw her forehead suddenly crease. A sudden movement. Unusual because she didn't feel like she was frowning. Lines appearing on her wedding day. Great.

She moved her fingers to her forehead to feel for the bumps but, bizarrely, her fingers did not comply in her reflection. Warning bells went off in her head.

'Lila,' she heard Grellie call.

She couldn't answer, she didn't want Grellie to hear her voice come from the spare bedroom. Suddenly she didn't want to explain anything. She'd made a mistake, she knew it. She'd always known Grellie was a rational woman, that her fears must have been for a reason. She'd always respected that, trusted it, however only then truly acknowledged it.

Startled, she stood upright. Her reflection was in sync then. She laughed, realising her imagination was playing up. She reached her hand out to touch the mirror.

'Lila, is everything okay up there?'

Suddenly the hand in the mirror turned, grabbed. She felt flesh, cold cold flesh, then she was pulled forcefully through the glass mirror, which felt like an icy blast of air on her skin. She was faced with herself, in a wedding dress. She looked to her right, the room was displayed back to her like a TV screen. The stark bed, with brass headboard, the dark, unworn floorboards. The white walls, the dusty bedside tables. A chair against the wall. That was it. An empty space where she had been standing. The door closed.

'Well, well, we finally meet in the flesh,' the girl opposite her said. She didn't sound like Lila and on further inspection didn't look exactly like her either. There was something missing behind the eyes.

They were dead, cold.

Lila looked around. The room in which she was standing was the exact reflection of the spare bedroom. Everything reversed. The picture the bed, the nightstands, the door.

'Lila!' she heard Grellie again.

'I'm here!' she heard her voice scream out. Desperation. Panic.

'She can't hear you,' the voice sang.

Lila turned to go back out of the mirror but she bumped against cold. Cold nothingness. A wall of cold.

'And you can't get out,' the sing-song voice continued.

'Who are you?' Lila finally spoke, anger and fear

causing her voice to tremble.

'Well today,' she looked down, 'it looks like I'm the bride. Da – da – da – da,' she sang and laughed.

'Who the hell are you?'

'Oh now, really, that upsets me. You look at me everyday and you don't see me?'

Lila's mouth opened, then closed, no idea what to say, her mind moving at the speed of light as she tried to figure it all out. Was it a hoax? Some cruel joke played by her friends on the morning of her wedding? But she knew it was not. It felt too real, she was not imagining this. Her natural instincts were telling her she was in serious danger.

'Well I see you everyday,' the girl continued. 'I look back at you everyday. You're not as perfect as you make yourself out to be, are you?' She smiled slyly.

'I want to get out of here,' Lila said, coldly now. 'Get me the hell out of here. Or else.'

'Or else what?' The girl smiled, happy with the challenge. 'Will you hurt me?'

Lila looked around the reversed room, her eyes scanning for weapons. She was well able to defend herself. You don't have a grandmother with no eyes, who is afraid of mirrors and hasn't left her home in over thirty years, living in a wild house on the tip of the headland, without learning how to defend yourself. Well she could and she would.

She looked around.

Her eyes fell upon one of the bedside lockers, and she remembered hiding a letter opener there after playing a game with a friend. She had been too afraid to bring it back downstairs in case Grellie knew she had the letter opener in her posession. So she had left it there, all those years. Lila headed straight for the locker, her trail sweeping the reflected dust along the floor, but none of it moved. She opened the drawer.

The girl threw her head back and laughed. 'What on earth are you doing?'

The drawer was empty. Inside was just a black hole, not even a bottom in the drawer.

'Don't you get it? They're just props. Nothing here is real. It's a *reflection*. It's not real.'

'Then you're not real,' Lila snapped back. 'That means that you are just a reflection, that you are nothing, that you are not real.'

'Lila, I'm the realest thing in here right now. I'm the only one who can get out of here.'

Lila swallowed.

'Lila!' Grellie called. Her voice was louder now, not just through urgency but because she was getting closer. Lila heard her footsteps on the stairs. She couldn't make up her mind whether she wanted Grellie to enter the room or not. She wouldn't though, she wouldn't know the sheet had been moved. Unless she felt her way, and she did not want Grellie to touch the glass.

'Here she is,' the girl said, raising an eyebrow, looking as though she were about to eat a banquet of food after a lifetime of starvation. 'I haven't seen that bitch for a long time. But I suppose she hasn't seen me either.' She giggled. 'You know you did well to listen to the old cow. You never looked in any of the mirrors ever. Twenty-eight years Lila. Why? Were you afraid?'

She didn't allow Lila to answer.

'But of all the days to disobey her.' She tutted as though Lila were a naughty child. 'The most important day of your life? Looks like I'll be the one sleeping with Jeremy tonight. I'll enjoy that.'

Lila couldn't help it. She reached out and slapped the girl hard across the cheek. The icy coldness of her cheek stung Lila's hand. The girl's head whipped to the side then back again. She held her hand to her cheek, then she started laughing.

'Well now I'm going to really enjoy it. Might even do it in front of a mirror, just so you can watch. Jeremy would like that, wouldn't he? Come to think of it, you would too. Vincent, was that his name? In the toilet? Honestly, Lila, I didn't know you had it in you. I wonder if Jeremy knows about him. Maybe a wedding night is a good night to confess all secrets.' She winked.

'If you think I'm going to let you take over my life you're wrong.'

'Of course. You don't think I'd just take your life without asking, do you? That'd just be rude.'

'Well then my answer is no.'

'I haven't asked you yet. You haven't heard the option. You have three chances to say yes.'

'There is no option. I'm going back through that mirror,' Lila said with steely determination.

'You can give me your eyes,' the girl said, deadly serious now.

'What? No!' Lila took a step away from her.

'Lila!' She heard Grellie again, anger in her voice now. 'Come here at once. Where are you?' She heard Grellie's bedroom door open. It would take her a while to feel around the room, realise she wasn't there.

'I'm here, I'm in here!' she yelled.

'She can't hear you,' the girl sang. 'Now give me your eyes.'

'No!' Lila shouted now. 'This is not funny. I want to get out of here. Let me out!'

The girl took a deep breath. 'You're not listening closely enough, Lila. You have one more chance.'

'Are you crazy? Why would I give you my eyes?'

'The price of freedom,' she said simply.

'Oh my god,' Lila whispered, her heart hammering. 'You took her eyes.'

'Yes, it's a bit messy,' the girl said screwing up her nose. 'Not very nice. That's why I refused when I was in your position, but your grandmother, she was clever. She chose freedom. I don't know about you though. You. You're vain. Might not do it. But you're my only chance. It's been a long time waiting. She hasn't made it very

33

easy for me.'

'How long have you been here?' Lila asked.

'I'm not here for polite chit-chat, Lila. I've been here long enough. Now you've one more chance.' She took a deep breath as though her life depended on it.

'You hurt my grandmother,' Lila said angrily. 'I will never let you do the same to me.'

'So what's the answer? Yes or no?'

'No,' Lila said defiantly.

The girl's face softened, she smiled and let out a long breath as though she'd been holding it for years.

'Thank you,' she said simply, her voice had softened too.

'What?'

'Take care. It gets cold in here. See you around.'

The girl stepped towards the mirror and in a rush of cold air she disappeared through to the other side. Lila chased her but once again slammed into a cold, icy nothingness. She watched as the girl looked at herself in the mirror. Lila felt herself automatically move in time with her. She fixed her hair when the girl did, wiped her smudged mascara when the girl did. She took a deep breath. Winked.

'I'm coming, Grandmother!' she called sweetly.

Grandmother, Lila heard. Grellie would know. Surely she'd know. Then the girl replaced the black sheet over the curtain and there was nothing. Absolutely nothing. Just blackness. The chair, the bed, the door, the picture, the bedside lockers. It was all gone. It was silent too, all she could hear was her own breathing. And it was cold.

Ellie was at her wits' end. She had searched everywhere, had felt all along the walls and floors of her bedroom in case Lila had collapsed. She was about to ring Jeremy when she had a thought. A desperate thought. She wouldn't have. God Almighty, please let her not have.

She felt her way along to the spare bedroom.

It was a long time since she had even passed through that door. A lifetime since she had entered it. She was a different woman then. Having inherited the house from her husband's mother, she had been exploring the place. They had just arrived, they were excited. Their first day in their first house together, they split up and looked at different rooms. She had chosen this one. He had left her after that. Her and her baby daughter. Couldn't deal with her after the incident. A nervous breakdown they'd called it. Self-harming.

She stood outside the door, her hand trembling as she reached out to touch the door knob. She felt nauseous. Her knees trembled so badly she could barely stand.

Then she heard the voice.

'I'm coming Grandmother!'

And she knew. She knew straight away. She felt sick.

The door opened.

A presence stood there, stood there watching her for a spell while she backed away and reached out for something to hold on to. To keep her up. A cold blast of air hit her. Then finally.

'What's wrong?'

Ellie, ever the survivor, pulled herself together. 'Lila, my dear,' she panted. 'My heart pills. Get me my heart pills.'

'What's wrong? Where are they? I've forgotten.'

'Remember what the doctor said,' Ellie continued.

'I know, I know you have to be careful. Where

are they?'

There was nothing wrong with her heart.

'My bathroom.'

She moved to Ellie's bedroom, a good guess that it was her room. She would have heard her feet move from the bedroom rug to the tiled bathroom floor but there was no sound. She was still in the bedroom.

'I can't find them.'

'Are you in the bathroom?'

'Of course.'

Ellie's test was complete, the girl wanted Ellie dead, she knew that. Well she didn't give up over fifty years ago, she wasn't about to start now.

She quickly made her way downstairs.

'Where are you going?' Lila asked, appearing at the stairs.

Panicking but trying to hide it Ellie reached the front door. She opened it knowing the car was at the end of the garden outside the gate.

'The driver's here, we have to go.'

'Oh,' her voice relaxed. 'Time to get married!'

'You go ahead to the car, I just want to make a phone call,' Ellie said easily.

'Who are you calling?' Lila was very quickly beside her. That cold air came with her.

'Jeremy. I just want to tell him we're leaving.'

'I'll come with you.'

She knew. She knew Ellie knew.

'Jeremy,' Ellie said, without excitement now, 'we're leaving the house now.'

'Is everything okay?' he asked, worried.

'Why?'

'You sound … you just sound down.'

Ellie left a silence. She wanted him to think there was something wrong. She wanted him to realise Lila wasn't standing beside him in the church.

'Grellie?'

'Yes?'

'Don't worry, you'll be okay. We'll take care of you today. Okay?'

Ellie swallowed hard. 'I'll see you soon.'

They didn't speak in the car. They didn't speak when they got out of the car. Then, just as they arrived at the church and the doors were pulled open, the girl whispered in Ellie's ear, 'Imagine, poor Lila stuck in that black nothingness all on her own. And look at us here.'

The wedding march started up.

Ellie whispered back, 'Yes, but she won't be there for long, so why don't you enjoy your moment and walk up the aisle alone.'

Ellie felt the girl's surprise. She had probably thought Ellie would go along with it but she wouldn't, she never would. Ellie stepped aside, had no idea where she was but felt the girl's presence disappear and knew she had taken the steps and was walking up the aisle.

Ellie felt someone guide her to a seat where she sat, her stomach sick, while she listened to the sermon. Jeremy with such emotion in his voice, her, the girl, with icy coldness in hers.

After the ceremony, Jeremy came to Ellie.

'Ellie, are you okay? Lila said you didn't feel well, that you couldn't walk her up the aisle.'

Ellie grabbed him by the arm, moved close to his ear, felt her nails dig in to his arm as she tried to hammer the message home. 'Jeremy listen to me, I know you think I am crazy–'

'Of course I don't think that,' Jeremy interrupted.

'Listen.' She dug her nails in harder. 'Fifty-two years ago, I looked in the mirror …' and she told him the story. When she had finished, she heard silence. 'Test her Jeremy. Just test her, that's all I'll say. Do it for me.'

'Okay, okay, Ellie.'

He didn't believe her, she knew that he didn't and she'd known that he wouldn't, but the seed had been planted and no matter how many years he would spend with this girl, at least he would always have Ellie's explanation in his head. Maybe some day he would believe it.

It was as though Lila had been standing in the middle of a football stadium without realizing it, because all of a sudden pitch-blackness changed to bright light and she had to adjust her eyes. She was surrounded by people, lots of people she knew and loved. She smiled at them all but her face wouldn't move. They had cameras in their hands, were smiling at her with fondness but they weren't looking at her, they were looking at another Lila, the girl, her reflection who was standing in the middle of the dance floor in Jeremy's arms.

Around her in the darkened space to which she was confined, everything she had spent the past few months organising was reflected back. The white roses on the tables were beautiful, the chairs were decorated with black bows. A black-and-white theme, all to disguise the black fabric that she had had specially made to cover the mirrors. But for some reason they were down on the floor.

And the girl was standing in the centre of the black-and-white dance floor, in Lila's dress, with her arms wrapped around Lila's boyfriend – husband now. And he was looking slightly bewildered. And Ellie … poor Ellie was standing among the crowd looking lost.

'What are you doing, Lila?' Jeremy asked through gritted teeth.

'Let's not fight now, everybody's staring.' The girl smiled back.

'Just tell me, why have you taken the drapes down?'

'What's the point in booking the ballroom if we cover up all these beautiful mirrors. I want to see myself.'

'It's for Ellie, not for you, you know that.'

'For who?'

Jeremy stiffened.

Then she laughed. 'Oh, of course, I know who you mean. How could I forget Grellie.' She laughed. 'Grellie, Grellie, Grellie, Ellie. Look, she'll get over it. She's acting so oddly today. I think we should take her to the doctor. She's rambling on about some bizarre things. She might have mentioned something to you.'

'About what?'

'About a mirror? Anything like that?'

Jeremy studied her. Felt her coldness. Knew something wasn't right. 'I love you, monkey.'

The girl laughed, was confused for a moment, then remembered earlier that morning when Lila had looked in the car mirror and said, 'I love you too, hippo.'

Jeremy smiled. Looked relieved.

'Now, let's dance.'

In the mirror, Lila suddenly felt her arms lift as they wrapped themselves around Jeremy's neck, though she couldn't feel him. Then she started to spin. Fast, then faster, round and round, till she felt sick. All around her, faces smiled and she wanted to call out for help, for them to get her out of here, but they weren't looking at her. Not in the mirror. They were looking at the girl in the centre of the floor.

Once home, Ellie stood in front of the mirror.

'I'm sorry, my love. I'm so sorry. I would swap places with you but it wouldn't work. I can't take your eyes. You would be my reflection and you would look like me. I've thought it all through. It won't work. I've called Jeremy over and over, but he's not answering. They went away, on the honeymoon … Oh my love, I'm so sorry.'

Ellie made plans to make the room prettier. She removed the black drape from the mirror. She added flowers to the room, opened the curtains, cleaned the room, lit the fireplace in an effort to warm up Lila's cold space, knowing that it wouldn't work but trying everything regardless. Months went by, Ellie wouldn't see anybody, she wouldn't take any visitors, refused to talk to Jeremy. She was afraid they'd take her away, and send her back to that place they locked her away in that very first time … So she stayed alone.

Then one day she had an idea. She wanted to paint the room, so she hired a local painter, took her time researching the local tradesmen. She found the right one.

A young man. Twenty-five years old. Polish, no family in the country.

'Here's your tea.' Ellie placed his mug down on the bedside locker.

'Thank you.'

'You're very welcome. Would you like any more sandwiches? Cakes?'

'No, thank you, I am full from all of the lovely food.' He smiled and patted his belly.

'Good. Do you mind if I ask a favour?' Ellie said politely.

He stopped painting and put down his brush.

'Would you please help me to clean this mirror? You seemed to have splashed it with some paint.'

He leaned in close to the mirror, placed a finger to the glass and tried to scrape it with his nail.'

'Now my love, this is your chance,' Ellie said.

Lila found herself faced with a young man. No more than twenty-five.

'What is this?' he asked, looking around, completely bewildered.

Lila's eyes were wide.

'I'm going to ask you a question,' she said coldly, 'and you have three chances to say yes …' She began.

The secret drifted on the breeze like a feather –
from the house, over the dandelions, thistles and
fuschia, out of the rusting gate, down the coastline
and into the village – about Ellie and her new
housemate. At first it was thought he was a lodger,
a young man helping the old blind woman around
the house now that her granddaughter had flown
the nest and curiously never returned. A
mysterious feud the villagers enjoyed playing
guessing games about without so much as coming
close to a whisper of the truth. They couldn't
understand the connection between the twenty-
five-year-old Polish man and the seventy-year-old
woman, but it appeared he brought her to life, and
she him, for there they lived until the old woman's
passing, happily together in the big house on the
cliff.

The Memory Maker

It is a beautiful day and she says so. He whistles as he walks alongside her and she hums along happily – a song played on the piano in the bar last night, which stays in their minds, trapped, the melody fluttering around continuously like a butterfly in a jam jar. Her hand in his, his so large his fingers wrap around her entire hand, giving her the appearance of a small child. She is not though, she is the most beautiful woman he has ever seen, has ever touched, has ever smelled. And he tells her so. She smiles, she has heard it a dozen times that morning but it does not annoy her; with each new compliment she glows even more so. He looks at her, with the sun streaming down on her blonde hair and she is lit up, a perfect angel. They walk through Merrion Square hand in hand, listening to the children's screams of delight, which float on the breeze, swept up from a nearby playground.

A *stick lands before their feet. She lets out a little high-
pitched yelp of fright, then she laughs at herself. He
teases her. A little embarrassed, she momentarily rests her
head on his shoulder. He smells her shampoo. Water lily.
Silly me, she says. He compliments her again. She is the
least silly woman he has ever seen, ever touched, ever
smelled. She takes the compliment again. A dog races by
them on the path, a blonde Labrador, large and clumsy
as though his feet don't belong to him at all, like he's
wearing an oversized pair of shoes. She says so and he
laughs. The dog dives on the stick, takes it in his hungry
mouth and races back in the direction he came. They
turn around and watch him scarper to his master. Eager
to please. Sorry, the man waves at them. No problem,
she replies. It's a beautiful day, she says to him, and he
agrees. They all agree. They continue on. It's deep in July,
the trees are crammed with leaves and flowers and the
air is filled with their scent. It tickles his nose, ignites his
hay fever. She hands him a handkerchief though he has
not yet sneezed. She knows him so well.*

He takes her handkerchief, fresh white, her initials sewn into the corner in pink. JJ. A gift from her mother. He blows his nose and playfully hands it back to her. She laughs again. The lines appearing around her mouth like the ripples in a pond after throwing a pebble. Light, fluid, natural, beautiful.

He is neither a doctor nor a scientist. Some consider him a psychologist, but he is not that either. He is merely a man who has loved, and for that he has acquired a wealth of experience, not just for what he does now and is known around the world for, but for his life.

Tucked away in the basement of a Georgian house in Fitzwilliam Square, the futuristic device finds its home in a historic setting. Dark rooms, despite large windows, and cold, damp furniture, despite constant heating. His clients are often surprised when they take in the surroundings. They didn't know what they were expecting, but it wasn't this. He is revered by some but angers most, for they fear that he has contaminated what is most natural in the world – the mind, the memory. And what has caused such debate around the world; what causes some people to adore him and some to curse him?

A device, a machine really. The memory-maker they call it. He doesn't. It's the mind that makes the memory – in his opinion it's more so the heart but he won't get into that now – and once the mind has made the memory, the machine stamps it into the memory files as though they are as real and true and as honest and unforgettable as all the others. The new memories are memories that people wish they had, or memories people have forgotten and need to refresh, though they never succeed in becoming the original thing no matter how hard they try to recreate them. The mind reinvents all by itself. It does it to survive. And the machine has helped the creator of the machine to survive. No, it hasn't helped him. It has *kept* him alive. Gave him reason. A thing he felt his life was deeply lacking in.

He came across the invention by accident. Contrary to popular opinion, he did not spend years working on the contraption, as a means of leaving behind the reality of what happened to him. The great sadness, which he has never discussed with anybody. And he doesn't believe that fate brought him to where he is now either. Nor does he believe in fate. Accidents happen. That's just what they are. Accidents. And so when he was playing around at home with his machines and wires and found a way to tell the machine to tell the brain to create a memory, it was an accident. Simple as that. But it was a convenient accident. Most aren't.

He has now perfected the machine and clients come from near and far to see him; frazzled, hopeless souls searching for peace of mind.

He knows when it's a journalist sitting before

him. He can see it in their eyes. A desire, just like regular clients, but the wrong kind. They are hungry. Though there are those with the intention to write positively about it and about him, he knows that most of them are intent on destroying what he has built up. Those people don't understand it. Some fear it, but most are too cynical to open their minds to its beauty. He doesn't care. He can spot them as soon as they step through the door, looking around with their questioning gaze – eyes searching him and his home and his machine like fire-drill interrogation. Their visits are never to self-improve, though each of them could do with the session for why would they hold such loathing for things that have nothing to do with them.

He is known for being particular about his visitors, for cancelling appointments at short notice, sometimes at the mere sight of them, closing the door on faces of anxious arrivees. He can sense the dishonesty, those who are merely there out of curiosity, those who wish to interrogate, replicate and obliterate. He doesn't want to share it. He doesn't want it to be misused.

He welcomes people from far and wide – the grieving, the sick, the lost, the occasional misplaced souls.

He realised some years ago that he had garnered quite a reputation. Word had spread about the device, rumours had spread about its creator, write-ups had appeared in the papers; personal accounts of customers, speculative pieces by those who hadn't set a foot near it or him or his building. He had shut up shop when he learned his machine was in fashion, angry that his work had been reduced to a fad. His desire was for the device to be for people who needed it, because to want it was merely not enough. It appeared that when he took it away, he gained more followers. He had a waiting list as long as Griffith Avenue, and dozens upon dozens of letters arrived each day, more than he could deal with. He reluctantly ended his solitary life and hired an assistant. A girl who called herself Judith, though he doubted that name was as much hers as the clothes on her back. Judith. It was a coincidence, he knew that. He didn't believe there was much more to it than that … she couldn't have known … and yet …

He had met her on Parliament Street, with City Hall and its three fronts of Portland stone behind him, the Liffey and the Four Courts ahead of him, as he strolled with cane in hand to yet another court date, as the forces – those who did not understand – attempted to stop his practice. He was representing himself then, knew what he was doing, left-over knowledge from his previous occupation. He'd passed her on the street. Judith that is. A brown little thing sitting on the pavement, a brown blanket wrapped tightly around her, her hair dark brown and slicked down with grease, her face heavily freckled as if each passing shoe had flicked her with dirt. She didn't even have an umbrella, the wet cold ground was slippy beneath feet and yet there she sat, on the only dry ground it seemed in the whole of Dublin.

He stopped beside her.

She looked up.

'Sir.'

'Would you like my umbrella?'

'You'll get wet.'

'But you're getting wet.'

'It's not my umbrella.'

'I'll give it to you.'

'You'll get wet.'

'I'll buy another one.'

He walked into the shop and purchased a new umbrella. A dull brown-and-olive plaid synthetic thing with a wooden handle, which looked as though a gust of wind would blow it inside out.

'Here.'

He handed her his umbrella. It was black, large, silk, with a sterling-silver handle. An eagle. It had been a gift. From the person he doesn't talk about. Can barely even think about. He didn't think twice about giving it away. He thought twice about not thinking twice. This intrigued him, made him wonder if he was healed after all this time. Then he thought of her face and her smell and her touch and his heart twisted and he knew the wound was as open and sore as it always was. She was not the umbrella; he was not giving her away.

'This is your umbrella.'

'Technically, they're both mine.'

'Why don't you give me the new one?'

'Why would I do that?'

'This is too good.'

'But I offered you this one.'

'But I don't mind the plaid one.'

'That's very kind of you but I'm a man of my word.'

She ran her hand over the handle. It was huge in her small hand.

'What's your name?'

A long pause. 'Judith.'

An accident. It was an accident. No signs. No such thing.

'Well, good day to you …' He couldn't say the name. Not yet.

He argued in court that day that hypnotists,

pyschologists and other alternative-medicinal practices should also be closed down on the same 'mind-altering' grounds he was being accused of. He questioned Dr Freud's theories of the unconscious mind, the defence mechanism of repression, his transference and his clinical practice of psychoanalysis, until they were all tired of listening to him. He altered peoples' minds no more than they. He won the case, though he would not know that until some weeks later.

The following day, he returned. It was not to see her, but because that was the route he must take. Though he had thought about her all night. He stopped beside her. She looked up.

'Did you forget your umbrella?' he asked.

'You mean your umbrella?'

'I gave it to you, it's no longer mine.'

'Well it's not mine either. I sold it.'

She wasn't sorry nor did he think she should be.

'Aren't you angry?'

'It was yours to do with as you wished. How much did you get for it?'

'A half-penny.'

He shook his head.

'You just said I could do as I wished,' she said, defensively.

'Indeed. But it was worth a great deal more.'

She shrugged.

'Well I needed a half-penny.'

He thought she needed a lot more than that.

'You don't have a cup.'

'A what?'

'A cup. For begging.'

'I'm not begging.'

'Then what are you doing?'

'I'm just sitting here.'

'Do people give you money?'

'Sometimes. Sometimes they give me umbrellas.'

He smiled. 'Would you like to work for me?'

'Doing what?'

'Administration. Taking in the post, reading letters, making appointments, that kind of thing.'

'Why?'

'I don't understand.'

'Why would you ask me?'

'Why not?'

She shrugged.

'If you think there's a reason why I shouldn't, you should be kind enough to tell me.'

She looked thoughtful, then looked him up and down and he got a sense of what her life must have been like up until the moment she met him. 'What do you want in return?'

'Nothing like that. Just exactly what I've asked you to do.'

She studied him for a long time. She appeared older then, her mind accessing the memories from which she has learned to make decisions.

'Okay.'

And so she began working for him. Others that saw her come and go assumed incorrectly that she was a housekeeper; company, though paid, marked the end to one aspect of the old man's self-appointed purgatory. But in reality she learned that the old man did not live an empty life, because it was filled to the brim with the ghost of his past with whom she worked alongside everyday.

She didn't know what he did initially but she learned as time went on and not from asking him questions. She never once asked if she could use the machine and he admired her for that because he could imagine there would be many memories she would like to change. She never asked him any questions and he didn't ask her any either. They were just two people who did what they did in the moment. They rarely spoke. She opened mail and without discussion he discovered she had learned his way of doing things. One evening, when she had left after the day's work, he sat at the table and read through the letters she had left behind. He took it up with her the following day.

'Why didn't you make an appointment for this man?' he asked.

He wasn't angry. He was never angry. He was merely interested and felt an answer would give him more of an insight into the workings of her own mind rather than why the man had not been granted an appointment.

She didn't look up as she hung her oversized coat on the hook on the back of the kitchen door and placed her – new – shoulder bag on the floor. She was looking much better these days.

'I didn't believe him.'

'But you don't know which letter I'm referring to.'

'I do. The man whose wife died in a road accident.'

He swallowed. 'Yes.'

'I didn't believe him.'

She looked at him pointedly then and he became a little flustered. Unusual for him and it was only slight, but it came over him all the same. He averted his eyes, was momentarily knocked off course, but if she noticed she didn't show it. She opened the large desk diary that he'd bought for her and looked through the appointments. He needed to cover up his obvious discomfort. He pointed to any letter on the table.

'And this woman, what about her?' He saw that his hand had a slight shake.

She sighed.

'Are you going to question every letter I refuse? Because if so, there's no point in my being here. You could just go back to doing this yourself.'

He nodded then stood. A cup of tea before the first appointment of the day. He placed a cup of tea, three sugars, lots of milk before her. She liked it in a mug, not a cup and saucer like he. He had to buy her one and this mug was the only one in

his home. He considered it hers.

'She writes gossip,' she said then, after taking a sip.

'Is that so?'

'I don't read it of course but I have seen her page before. A high-society woman. She finds everything a nuisance.' She put on a fancy accent. 'Writes about who is seen having afternoon tea with whom. I didn't think you would want her here.'

He nodded.

'I won't ask you any more.'

The office was the kitchen. Judith based herself there from eight a.m. until four p.m. every day. She rarely moved from her chair at the table, never looked around, rooted in the drawers, barely looked up from her desk diary to take in her surroundings. She sat on her chair at the table with the letters and the appointment book as though it was the driest part of the room.

The door bell rang. He opened it to a young man in a suit, dark circles under his eyes, a sensible hair cut, cleanly shaven, aftershave emanating from his skin in waves. He was a banker of some sort, an accountant. Something to do with numbers and straight lines. He removed his fedora hat and looked left, right, and both again before stepping inside, nervous to be seen at this address.

He stepped away from the doorway to welcome the man in.

'My name is Jack Collins.'

'Yes.'

He left the door open and turned and walked down the hall for him to follow. Jack hesitated at the door, rethinking the entire situation. How much did he really need to be here? He took in the empty hallway, the original tiles, some cracked, faded, a smell of mould that any amount of bleach and spray could not remove, the bare walls and he stepped inside.

Jack followed the old man into a small room. A machine. The machine. Two old armchairs. A

fireplace. Unlit. It smelled of damp. It felt cold.

'Take a seat.'

The old man was already sitting down.

Again, Jack hesitated, weighing up his options. Then he sat.

Jack placed his briefcase on the thin cold carpet and looked around for a place to lay his hat. The old man offered no help. He settled on hanging it from the handles of his briefcase. He opened the button of his suit jacket, leaned forward, his elbows on his knees as though about to negotiate a deal and he didn't want the fireplace to hear him. A salesman, the man guessed.

'So,' Jack said.

'So, I attach these here.' He ignored the impending small talk and attached three wires with suction pads to the man's temples, and forehead. The mind's eye.

'Begin,' he said, not looking Jack in the eye. Waiting.

'What do I do?'

'You just describe the memory as best you can, colours, smells, sounds, expressions of those around you. Speak clearly please.'

'How does this work?' Suddenly he looked unsure. Not of himself but of the machine. Of the hype surrounding it.

Did it ever matter how it worked? The old man had debated this endlessly in the beginning years. It was like before turning on the wireless wanting to be told how exactly it works. Or before getting into an automobile wanting to know the exact workings of its engine. It never mattered. 'Do you want me to tell you how it works or do you just want it to work?'

Once again Jack hesitated. He studied the old man, not liking his attitude, not having imagined it would be like this at all. An old machine in a damp, run-down room with an old man with a chip on his shoulder. It was short of magical. But he seemed to question his predicament again and then surrendered.

Jack cleared his throat.

'I was away at the weekend. Or at least I told my wife I was.'

He paused for a reaction. He didn't get one. The old man didn't flinch, didn't react, didn't appear to judge.

'In fact I didn't leave the city.'

Again no reaction. He sighed.

'I met someone and I've never done it before but I …' his voice cracked slightly. 'I can't sleep, I can't eat. I know I made a huge mistake. But I know I can't lie, I just can't. Every time she looks at me I just know she knows. She asks me about the weekend away, the one I was supposed to have and I just freeze, I get confused. I want to close my eyes and make it all go away, I want to see the weekend I should have had.'

They mistook him for a counsellor all the time. That's not what he was there for.

'Do you need to know all this?' Jack asked, his eyes wet.

'No.'

'Why didn't you tell me?'

'I thought you were getting to it. You just need to tell me the memories.'

'The ones I want to put in my mind?'

The man nodded. 'And you know this does not erase memories, it merely adds new ones. I'm not in the business of deleting memory files.'

'I know that.'

Jack moved his hat to the armchair rest, reached into his briefcase and retrieved a brochure.

'This is where I should have been. A sales conference. In a hotel in Kerry. That is the hotel there. That is the bedroom. They have extensive grounds, with views over Kenmare Bay. I would have spent time walking there. I enjoy walking. The climate enables a subtropical woodland to grow. They have eucalyptus trees. The air smells sweet. Fresh.' He swallowed. 'My colleague told me about it.'

The old man motioned for him to continue.

'The sales conference was in the hotel. That I don't need help with, it's just another conference room in another hotel. But there was a tour around the Ring of Kerry. My wife always wanted to take that trip. I should take her but I can't now. She'll realise I've never been there but maybe after this …' He looked at the old man again needing encouragement to continue. The man helped him go through the finer details, how the clouds cast shadows on the mountains, how the air smelled fresh from eucalyptus, sweet with rhubarb, and salty from the sea, how he felt the sun on his face, how his room looked, how he had no cash to tip the man who brought his luggage to his room, how his shirt was crumpled when he took it out of his case, how he should have put it in a suitbag just as his wife had said. They talked about how he'd bought her and the children presents not from Dublin's Grafton Street on the way home from his city-centre hotel, but from the railway station as he awaited his delayed train. How he'd phoned his wife the bathing pools during a break in their conference instead of when the woman he was with had momentarily left his side in bed in that city hotel.

When Jack was finished the man removed the pads from his forehead and temples. Jack blinked a few times then looked back at him.

'Goodness.'

The old man turned the machine off. Jack seemed relieved, jovial, cocky even.

'Saved me money on travel, that did. Should have said I was in Fiji.'

The old man stood up and began his goodbyes. 'Yes, well, it sounds like it would have been a beautiful trip. Shame you didn't go on it.'

Jack's smile faded.

They are nearing the gateway of the park. Out of the green oasis and back to the concrete city, though he doesn't mind. It's a beautiful day. The best day of the year, they wonder. They walk under the trees, a light chill now as they are sheltered from the sun. She shivers slightly and he holds her hand tighter as though by doing so he can keep her warmer. He wants to make everything perfect for her all of the time, even when he knows it's impossible. The smell of moss fills his nose, tickles again. The damp floor to which the sun's rays can't creep is thick in the air. It is refreshing and they say so. He steps aside to allow her to walk through the gate before him. She thanks him and waits for him to join her. They look at one another, prepare to part and already his stomach churns at having to leave this dream and go about his work day.

Thanks for last night, she says. There is a shyness about her now, though not an ounce of it last night. He loves this about her but he does not say. He doesn't want to make her uncomfortable. They make arrangements to meet again tonight. Dinner in the Shelbourne perhaps. Yes. That would be nice. Perhaps an early night. She laughs again, the shyness gone. Of course, my dear. Of course.

'A cheating husband?' he said to Judith as soon as Jack Collins had left.

She didn't look up.

'He loves his wife.' She sounded bored by it. But the boredom was too forced. He knew she cared.

'So he said.' He sighed.

'You didn't believe him?'

'I did.'

'But you don't approve of him?'

He didn't want to answer. He wasn't supposed to judge his clients. He never usually did.

'Everyone deserves a second chance,' she said.

'I'm not in the business of helping people lie.'

She looked up then. He saw doubt.

'Making new memories is not lying,' he said a little too forcefully. 'That appointment was a

mistake,' he said, more gently.

'Okay,' she shrugged.

He sat with Judith. They ate cheese sandwiches as she continued to read through the letters. He watched her but tried not to make it obvious. Her facial expression didn't change. He couldn't tell whether she was impressed or not by any letter her eyes moved over. She put them into two separate piles. He tried to figure out which was which pile. She finished another letter, took a bite of her sandwich then put the letter in the pile on the left. He still couldn't tell.

There was never any conversation, but never any awkwardness either. Their previous conversation about Jack was about as long or as intense as it had ever reached. He realised then that he rather enjoyed her company, he who had spent the last forty-one years on his own. He realised that he quite looked forward to her morning arrival, that for the few hours after she left, he felt … well, he missed her. The house was hollow again. Carved out like a tree. Now he felt he was waiting, always had an expectant feeling, for someone to arrive, for something to happen. He hadn't wished that for a long time. That feeling had long since been with him. He stopped chewing, put his sandwich down.

She didn't look at him. 'What?'

She ripped open an envelope.

He didn't say anything.

She looked a little uncomfortable.

'I'm trying to discern which pile of letters is the

one which moves you beyond belief.'

She looked at him then, aware he'd made a joke. Then she stabbed a finger on the pile on the left. 'This one.'

He smiled. He wouldn't have known but it made him feel good. He may not bore her entirely. He looked at his pocket watch; he always left an hour between appointments. He only saw two people a

day, sometimes one depending on the memory. He returned to the machine.

'It's been twenty-five years since he died,' Mrs de Lacey spoke with her neck arched out like a swan, her skin stretching and pulling tight around her muscles. The pearls on her necklace nestled into the dips in her craned neck. She was trying to appear strong but he could sense that she was flapping wildly below the surface.

'I can remember lots of things about him, lots of things we did together, lots of things he said but—' And now her resolve weakened, her tough exterior crumbled just a little. He neck shortened, her skin loosened, her shoulders lapsed and she appeared to fall in on herself, sobbing.

'Mummy.' Her daughter reached out and touched her mother's arm, surprised and more than a little embarrassed by the display of emotion.

He didn't say anything.

The daughter looked at him uncomfortably, as if he had the ability to stop the water works.

'But his face,' her mother continued, truly sobbing now, forcing the words out whether anybody liked it or not. 'His face when I close my eyes.' She closed her eyes. 'I can't see him. I just can't.'

'Mummy, just stop now. What on earth are you talking about? Give yourself a moment to compose yourself.' Her daughter's cheeks were flushed.

'It's like a blur,' she continued, her eyes streaming. 'I can see him but not closely, not exactly and he keeps changing. Changing age, changing expression. I can't seem to hold on to one memory, to one perfect moment.'

The daughter rummaged in her handbag.

'Here, Mummy.' She shoved a handkerchief into her clenched, angry hands. 'Your nose,' she said, with a little disgust.

'I know what his eyes look like, I know his lips.' She touched her own lips sensually, remembering. The daughter looked away, shocked, further embarrassed. 'But all together I can't see him. It's like I'm looking too close, I need to move further back, to see the entire picture.'

She squeezed her eyes shut, wrinkles tense. Then she opened them again, disappointed he wasn't there.

She looked at him then for the first time. 'I want to be able to remember him at any moment I so please. He's all I've got.'

'Mummy.' The daughter's face fell. 'You have us.'

'Oh don't be silly, Lizzie, you all argue about whose turn it is to take me out for lunch and I know you're not all arguing to take me out. No, he's up there, the only place I have him,' she said jabbing her finger against her temple roughly, against her tough old skin, as if stubbing out a cigar. 'And I'm losing him.'

Lizzie cleared her throat. 'I have a photograph of him.'

He took it. An imposing black-and-white photograph of an overweight man wearing a monocle, hands clasped on his lap, staring coldly into the camera. Behind him on the wall was the head of a stag.

'That's our hunting lodge,' she said rather proudly.

'No, no, no.' Mrs de Lacey waved the photograph away as though it were a wasp. 'That's not him.'

'Mummy, that was taken right after he became president of the cricket club, I know so because look, his lapel —'

'I don't want to remember a damn cricket-club or hunting-lodge photograph,' she snapped, and once again her daughter appeared shocked, wounded even. 'I want to remember him as he was in the morning, first thing when I opened my eyes. I want to see him as we made love.' She closed her eyes then, savouring a moment.

'Mummy,' her daughter said, shocked, but she'd softened, as though all of a sudden seeing her mother as a woman.

'When he first held Ellis when he was born, playing with the children in the garden. The way his nostrils twitched when he was angry.' She laughed then. 'I know all these things about him, but when I close my eyes I can't see them any more.'

He placed the pads on her temples and forehead, he attached the wires to the machine. He switched it on.

'So paint me the picture and that's what you'll see.'

He runs his fingers through her hair, it's loosely curled and his fingers fall straight through it, it is so soft, like velvet. He hears his name being called. A colleague to his right-hand side coming toward him. He greets him.

She tells him she'll see him later. He is a little distracted but he agrees. He quickly brushes his lips against the skin on her fingers. Her skin is warm and soft. She takes her hand away quickly so as not to embarrass him in the company of his colleague, and she moves away. He turns to greet his colleague. They begin to discuss a case that has been boggling the offices for a great many months. He hears her call goodbye again but he is caught in conversation, she will understand, he will see her later. He hears a sound. A God-awful sound. A sound he will never forget. Never forget. His colleague grabs his arm so tightly, he feels nails on his skin through his summer suit. And he knows but he cannot look. He does not want to have to remember that sight for the rest of his life, for he knows he will see it everyday. In waking hours and in sleep. Every single day.

When Judith arrived at his home the following morning her brown hair was covering her face. Her eyes were cast down, wouldn't meet his gaze. With her chin down she pushed passed him in the hallway and made her way to the kitchen. She stalled when she reached the door and saw the table. He had prepared breakfast for the first time. A feast of sausages, eggs, tomato, pudding – black and white – mushrooms of all different sizes. A rack of toast sat in the middle of the table with every condiment imaginable. He quite literally did not want her to have to ask for anything.

She swayed a little and he rushed forward to catch her but her small pink hand appeared from her oversized coat sleeve and she held on to the door frame. That's when she turned and he saw. Her eye. Her left eye was bruised, the flesh around it had swollen up so much you would barely know an eye was buried beneath. Her skin had the appearance of a rotten peach. She saw his face, the look in his eye and she turned around again quickly. Anger surged through him. Never had so much anger rushed through his blood since Judith. His Judith. And now this Judith. His Judith, he realised. His grip tightened around his cane, his knuckles turned white.

He wanted to say so many things – shout, demand to know who did this to her. So many questions and feelings he had inside he had to take a minute to process which one he should say first. The wrong thing and he knew she'd be gone. She was so fragile, her presence so precious but like a feather, a light wind and he knew she'd be taken away from him so easily. He managed to calm himself a little. The red-faced anger had left him and now he felt the tremble in his body, the aftershock. He cleared his throat to speak but she stopped him. Her pink hand jerked suddenly into the air to halt him as a traffic warden would. The sleeve fell further down in the motion and he saw the markings on her wrist. Yellow-tinted black bruises all the way up her arm.

'Don't,' she said, and her voice was firmer than he'd ever heard.

He didn't.

He knew he would not.

He would not risk losing her.

'Don't ask,' she said, 'and I won't ask why you've done this, this morning.'

He was suddenly embarrassed but understood. He nodded, knowing with her back turned she couldn't see him but her comment was not a question and she expected no answer.

They sat at the table, his jubilant mood from that morning murdered, and they ate in silence. She didn't eat much. Neither did he.

His first client of the day arrived. An eighteen-year-old whose father, he said, despised him. He wanted memories of spending time with his father so that when he looked at him he wouldn't feel so sad about what he was missing and what he had missed. His father in the stand at his football match, his father cheering when he'd scored the winning goal. His father smiling when he made a joke. No new conversations, nothing dramatic and exotic. Just memories with his father just being there. Present and attentive.

He was afraid she wouldn't come back the next day but she did. As usual she was dressed in a day dress but this had long sleeves and a high neck with back buttons to hide what he had seen before. But it was too late. He would see it for ever. Whenever he closed his eyes. The flesh around the eye had coloured more. And for weeks it went back to being as it was before, only it wasn't like it was before. It was polluted, their fresh perfect existence together polluted, until late one night she arrived doubled over and coughing on his doorstep, so much blood he couldn't see where it was coming from. She wouldn't let him call the police or bring her to the hospital. She wouldn't even let him clean her up. She wanted to do it herself, she just needed a place. She locked herself in the bathroom and was in there for an hour, the sound of running water and occasional splashing the only thing to let him know she was still alive.

She opened the door, dressed in his shirt, looking like a small child in the oversized striped top. She slept in his bed, he slept – or didn't – on the couch. They never spoke of it, though he had

to fight with himself not to. A few days later she came to him.

'Can we talk?'

'Of course. I have an appointment now. Would you like to wait in the kitchen?'

'I am your appointment.' She sat before him in the armchair.

He suddenly froze.

'I'm not going to tell you anything,' she said.

He nodded just once, not trusting himself to speak just then.

'I know you're not a psychiatrist. I know that you hate people telling you things.'

'You're different.'

She smiled sadly. 'So here is my memory. The one that I want. The day I arrived here.'

He knew which day she meant.

'You open the door, you're happier than I've ever seen you. I'm intrigued but I smile. Your smile is so big it's contagious. You're happy to see me smile. Good morning, Judith, you say. My name is Mary, I tell you.'

She was looking at him intently, her eyes shining with tears.

Mary, he thought, what a beautiful name.

'Mary, you say, that's a beautiful name. Thank you I say. Then you bring me down the hall, you take my coat, always the perfect gentleman, and you show me the kitchen. As soon as you have opened the door the smell hits me. It's the most beautiful table of food I've ever seen. It's the most thoughtful thing anyone has ever done for me.

'And I turn around to face you and I thank you.

And I tell you that there is the most beautiful smell, the most beautiful spread, the most thoughtful thing anyone has ever done for me.

'And you are so happy.

'We sit down and I eat everything. I eat everything because it tastes so good and I want you to know that I appreciate how long it must have taken you to cook it. And I tell you it's the tastiest food I've ever eaten.

'And you're so happy.

'Then you read the newspaper and we talk about the news stories. I ask you to explain, not because I want to know but because I want to hear your voice. Because I love the sound of your voice. Because it's the most solid and safe thing I've ever heard in my life. The most solid thing in my whole life.'

His eyes well up.

'And I tell you that and you almost cry. And then I ask you about the machine, about how you did it. But I don't ask why, even though I've always wanted to know why. I can guess. I've heard the stories of what happened, but I don't believe them all. But I don't ask you why because now I understand. I already know why. Because I know how a moment can pass – how you've really wanted to say something to someone or do something, but something happens and you don't, and you almost want to explode afterwards because you didn't do it. And I know you get annoyed when people come in here and try to make stupid memories like becoming sporting heroes and play around on their wives with prettier women. Because that's not what it's about. It's about fixing a moment back to the way it should have been, had you not got distracted, or if you weren't such a coward or if you had known that that lost moment was the only moment you had to say or do what you wanted.

'But I don't say that to you then, because you know that I know. We talk about the appointments. We have a cheese sandwich. Before I go, I thank you for everything you've done for me. And I give you a hug. And it's the warmest, softest – safest – hug I've ever had and I know that you'll protect me through everything.'

He nods.

'And then I go home. Happy. And you watch me leave. Happy. And we both know that we're going to be okay.'

She stopped then, tears streaming down both their faces. She removes the wires from her head, she stands, takes her bag and coat, and leaves. The front door clicks behind her. He watches her boots on the metal steps upstairs to the roadside. All he can hear is the hum of the machine. He never sees

her again.

He puts the pads over his temples and forehead.

He runs his fingers through her hair, it's loosely curled and his fingers fall straight through it, it is so soft, like velvet. He hears his name being called. A colleague to his right-hand side coming toward him. He greets him.

She tells him she'll see him later. He is a little distracted but he agrees. He quickly brushes his lips against the skin on her fingers. Her skin is warm and soft.

She takes her hand away quickly so as not to embarrass him in the company of his colleague, and she moves away. He turns to greet his colleague. They begin to discuss a case that has been boggling the offices for a great many months. He hears her call goodbye again but he is caught in conversation. He tells his colleague he is very sorry but he must say goodbye to her properly. His colleague is a little put out but he waits for him. He looks up and she turns around and their eyes meet, she smiles at him. He smiles back. One final confirmation of their love.

He hears a sound. A God-awful sound. A sound he will never forget. Never forget. His colleague grabs his arm so tightly, he feels nails on his skin through his summer suit. And he knows but he cannot look. He does not want to have to remember that sight for the rest of his life, for he knows he will see it everyday. In waking hours and in sleep. Every single day.

It is not the memory he needs to change, it was almost perfect. It was the most perfect day of his life up until that point. But Mary is right, it is what he regrets, what beats him up inside that makes him relive it over and over a thousand times a day. If he had just looked up when she called. They would have smiled, she would have seen his love one last time. The horse and carriage would always have hit her. The horse was frightened by something else. It bolted. He can't change each thing that happened to each person around the square that day. He can't bring her back to life in his mind, it would be pointless. But that last look, that's what he wishes to change. It was the only error on both of their parts that day. The accident ... that was somebody else's error. Then it would all have been one hundred

per cent perfect – until that point.

He turns the machine off. The humming stops. And there is nothing.

Acknowledgments

Thanks to my family, Marianne Gunn O'Connor and the wonderful HarperCollins team, especially my editors Lynne Drew and Kate Burke.